The Good Little Bad Little Pig!

This edition published by
Parragon Books Ltd in 2014

Parragon Books Ltd
Chartist House
15–17 Trim Street
Bath BA1 1HA, UK
www.parragon.com

Written by Margaret Wise Brown
Illustrated by Loretta Schauer
Edited by Catherine Allison
and Robyn Newton
Designed by Kathryn Davies
Production by Charlene Vaughan

ISBN 978-1-4723-4524-0
Printed in China

The Good Little Bad Little Pig!

PaRragon

Bath • New York • Cologne • Melbourne • Delhi
Hong Kong • Shenzhen • Singapore • Amsterdam

One day, a little boy called Peter asked his mother if he could have a pig.

"What!" said Peter's mother.

"You want a dirty little, bad little pig?"

"No," said Peter. "I want a clean little pig. And I don't want a bad little pig or a good little pig. I want a good little, bad little pig."

"I've never heard of a clean little pig," said
Peter's mother, "but let's try to find one."
So they sent a letter to a farmer
who owned some pigs:

The farmer had five little pigs who lived in an old, muddy pigpen with an old mother sow.

When Peter's mother saw the pig, she said,
"What a dirty little pig!"
The pig said,

"Squeeeeeeeeeee-ump-ump-ump!"

But Peter said, "Wait till he's
had a bath."

But then the little pig jumped out of the box and ran around, squealing like a fire engine.

"What a bad little pig!" said Peter's father and his grandmother.

"He is not a bad little pig," said Peter. "Wait until he gets to know us."

The little pig stared at Peter out of his little eyes. Then he shook himself and trotted after Peter.

"What a good little pig!" said Peter's grandmother, and she gave the little pig a bowl of bread and milk to eat. "Wait," said Peter. "Remember, this is a good little, bad little pig."

"Galump-gump gump gump gump."

The little pig made snuffling, sneezing noises as he ate.

"What terrible table manners!" said Peter's grandmother. "What a bad little pig!"

"Come on, you good little, bad little pig," said Peter. "I will give you a bath."

Peter put the little pig into a bath of warm water and rubbed him with a big bar of white soap. "What a mess!" said Peter's mother. "What a bad little pig!"

Peter scrubbed and rubbed until the pure
white soapsuds were all black and the little pig
was all clean from the tip of his tail to the tip of
his nose.

Then, Peter took the little pig for a walk.

"Look," said Peter to the policeman. "Did you ever see such a fine little, clean little pig?"

"No," said the policeman. "What a good little pig." He blew his whistle and stopped all the cars so that Peter and the little pig could cross the road.

The little pig did not want to cross the road. Peter pulled on the lead, but the little pig refused to budge.

The people in their cars
began to honk their horns.

So the policeman pushed and Peter pulled the pig into the road.

"Squeak-squeeeeeeee-ump-ump-ump!"

Then, suddenly, the little pig trotted on, as nice as you please. "What a good little pig," said the people in the cars as they went on their way.

And so it was that Peter got just what he wanted.
A **good** little, **bad** little pig.

Sometimes the little pig was good
and sometimes he was bad,

but he was **the best** little pig
a little boy could **ever** have.

EVER!

Oink!